For my dad, who squirreled away a
basement full of whatchamajiggers.
—K. D.

To Betty
—K. L.

Ω

Published by
PEACHTREE PUBLISHING COMPANY INC.
1700 Chattahoochee Avenue
Atlanta, Georgia 30318-2112
www.peachtree-online.com

Text © 2021 by Kathleen Doherty
Illustrations © 2021 by Kristyna Litten

The illustrations were rendered in pencil, ink textures, and digital.

Printed in November 2020 by Leo Paper in China
10 9 8 7 6 5 4 3 2 1
First Edition
ISBN: 978-1-56145-959-9

Cataloging-in-Publication Data is available from the Library of Congress.

THE THINGITY-JIG

Written by **Kathleen Doherty**

Illustrated by **Kristyna Litten**

Ω

PEACHTREE

ATLANTA

One night, under the light of a silvery
moon, all of Bear's friends were deep
asleep.

But Bear wasn't sleepy—he wanted to play.
So he wandered off to find some fun in
people town.

Tap. Poke. Sniff.

Bear nosed around until he found...

a **Thingity-Jig**.

It looked friendly. Bear plopped

down on its lap.

Bingity.

The **Thingity-Jig** was a springy thing.

A bouncy thing. A sit-on-it, hop-on-it,

jump-on-it thing.

Bear hurried home to tell his friends.

Bing.

Boing!

"Wake up! Wake up! I found something fun—a bouncy, springy **Thingity-Jig**!"

Rabbit opened one eye.

"Really?"

"This **Thingity-Jig** will be sit-on-it, hop-on-it, jump-on-it fun...," said Bear. "And I need help bringing it home."

"Not now, Bear." Fox yawned.

"We're sleeping."

"Wait till morning," grumbled Raccoon.

But Bear wasn't sleepy—he wanted to play. So he took matters into his own paws.

He'd bring the **Thingity-Jig**

home all by himself.

But how?

It was too heavy to carry.

Too hard to push.

But not too big to roll.

Smack. Wallop. Whack.

Under the light of a silvery moon,

Bear went to work. He clinked and

clanked until he built...

a **Rolly-Rumpity!**

It was a draggy thing. A pully thing.

A pack-it-up, heap-it-up, load-it-up thing.

It was just what Bear needed to wheel home

the **Thingity-Jig**. But Bear found it *impossible* to lift

the **Thingity-Jig** onto the **Rolly-Rumpity**.

He dashed home.

"Wake up! Wake up! I need your help.

Then we'll climb and jump."

"Jump?" Rabbit wiggled her nose.

"I like to climb." Fox rubbed his eyes.

"But right now, I need to sleep."

Raccoon groaned. "Rest first, jump later."

But Bear wasn't sleepy—
he wanted to play. So...

Smack.

Wallop.

Whack.

Under the light of a silvery moon,
Bear fiddled and whittled until he
built...

a **Lifty-Uppity!**

It was a boosty thing.
A hoisty thing. A pick-it-up,
raise-it-up, jack-it-up thing.

Bear managed to haul the **Thingity-Jig**

onto the **Rolly-Rumpity**.

Yippee-doo! Things were working out!

But on his way back, Bear took the

zigzag way, and the **Rolly-Rumpity** got

stuck in the mud. Bear ran home

"Wake up! Wake up!" Bear shouted.

"I need your help. Then we'll bounce and hop."

"I like to hop!" Rabbit flicked her ears.

"Maybe when the sun comes up." Fox leaned back and stretched.

"Go away, Bear," griped Raccoon.

Bear *had* to play. Nothing could get in his way. He wanted that **Thingity-Jig**. And he wanted it NOW. So...

Smack.

Wallop.

Whack.

Under the light of a silvery moon, Bear thunked and thwacked to build...

a **Pushy-Poppity.**

It was quite the contraption!

Bear used the **Pushy-Poppity**

to free the **Lifty-Uppity**

that raised the **Rolly-Rumpity**

that wheeled the **Thingity-Jig**

all the way home.

At daybreak, Bear flumped the

Thingity-Jig down with a loud THUMP.

His friends sat up with a start. They stared

at the **Thingity-Jig**, and it stared back.

"This is a **Thingity-Jig**," said Bear.

"You can bounce and hop. And leap
and climb. You can even do a flip-flap,
springy-ding flop."

His friends jumped
to their feet.

"WHOOPEE!" they cried.

"Let's bounce and hop!"
said Rabbit.

"And leap and climb!" said Fox.

"And springy-ding flop!"
said Raccoon.

Springity.

Sproing.

WHEE!

Bear clapped and cheered.

"My turn!"

"We need more time,"
begged Rabbit.

Bear waited and
watched.

He shifted from one foot
to the other.

"Just a little longer,"
said Fox.

Bear let out
a big huff.

"Thank you," said Bear.

And he flopped down on

the **Thingity-Jig**.

Bingity...

Bing...

Boing.

Under the light of a golden sun,

Bear curled up in the arm

of the **Thingity-Jig**.

Snorty-snore.

Zzzz...